A School for AMOS

If you enjoy reading this book, you might also like to try another story from the **MAMMOTH STORYBOOK** series:

A School for AMOS

Elana Bregin

illustrated by *Sharon Lewis*

mammoth

First published in Great Britain in 1997
by Mammoth, an imprint of Reed International Books Ltd
Michelin House, 81 Fulham Road, London SW3 6RB
and Auckland and Melbourne

Text copyright © 1997 Elana Bregin
Illustrations copyright © 1997 Sharon Lewis

The rights of Elana Bregin and Sharon Lewis to be identified as the author
and illustrator of this work have been asserted by them in accordance with
the Copyright, Designs and Patents Act 1988

ISBN 0 7497 3101 X

10 9 8 7 6 5 4 3 2 1

A CIP catalogue record for this book
is available from the British Library

Printed in Great Britain by Cox & Wyman Ltd,
Reading, Berkshire

Contents

~

One

Amos Gumede is very excited. Today he is going to school.

He has a new suitcase.

A pencil.

An exercise book.

But no uniform yet.

'I want to go to school with you!' cries his small sister, Thembi.

'I also want to go,' barks his dog, Pavement.

'No, you must stay here,' Amos tells them. 'School is for big children. Not little girls and dogs. When I come home again, I will teach you what I've learnt.

'Come, Amos,' says Gogo, his grand-mother. 'We must hurry up or we will be late for registration.'

Gogo is taking Amos to school today. His mother can't go because she has to work in Mrs Botha's house, cleaning and cooking.

Amos puts on his best black shoes. He waves goodbye to Thembi and Pavement. He picks up his suitcase and follows Gogo out of the house.

He feels very important. He is the first person in his family to go to school.

His mother has had no education.

His grandmother can't read or write.

His father, who is dead now, also never went to school.

Amos has heard President Mandela, who the people call Madiba, speaking on TV. 'Education is very important,' he said. 'All children must go to school. They must learn so that they can be clever and know things.

In the new South Africa, education is for all.'

The school where Gogo and Amos are going is just round the corner. Before, only white children were allowed to go there. But now, it is open to all.

When they arrive, they find a lot of people already waiting, wanting to register their children for Class One.

They have to stand in a long line to see the headmaster. The line moves very slowly.

Amos sits on his new suitcase and dreams of all the things he will learn in Class One.

At last, it is their turn to go into the headmaster's office.

'I'm sorry,' the headmaster says to

Gogo, 'but there is no place for Amos in this school. You will have to register him somewhere else.'

Amos is very disappointed. He feels like crying. But Gogo says, 'Never mind, we will try the next school. I am sure we will get a place for you there.'

The next school is quite a bit further away. They take a bus there. Amos likes

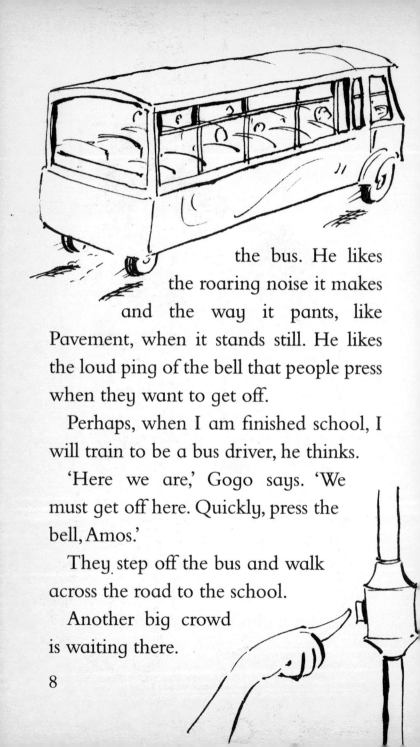

the bus. He likes the roaring noise it makes and the way it pants, like Pavement, when it stands still. He likes the loud ping of the bell that people press when they want to get off.

Perhaps, when I am finished school, I will train to be a bus driver, he thinks.

'Here we are,' Gogo says. 'We must get off here. Quickly, press the bell, Amos.'

They step off the bus and walk across the road to the school.

Another big crowd is waiting there.

They have to get into line again.

The sun is hot and Amos is thirsty. He worries about Gogo who has bad legs and can't stand for too long.

Their turn comes to see the headmistress.

'I am very sorry,' she says. 'We are full up here. You will have to take Amos to another school. Try Park Street Primary. Maybe they have some places left.'

Park Street Primary is much further away.

Amos and Gogo have no more money for the bus. So they have to walk.

They walk and walk.

It is nearly lunch-time when they

arrive. There are no crowds waiting. They can go straight in to see the headmaster.

'I'm sorry,' he says. 'Our school is full already. We are not taking any more children.'

'Please,' begs Gogo. 'This is the third school we have tried. Please, can't you make a place for Amos?'

'I'm very sorry,' says the headmaster. 'Our classes have too many children already. We can't fit in even one more.'

'It's too late to look for more schools now,' Gogo says to Amos. 'We'll have to go home and try again tomorrow.'

Home is a very long way from where they are.

They have to walk slowly and rest often, because Gogo's legs are worrying her. It's nearly dark when they reach their thin house on the hillside. Amos is very tired. His feet hurt from all the walking. His stomach hurts from hunger. But his heart hurts most of all.

His mother sees his sad face and gives him a big hug. 'Don't worry, Amos,' she says. 'We will find a school for you.

Madiba has promised us that all children will get an education. Somewhere, there must be a school with a place for you.'

She cooks a delicious supper of chicken and rice and beans. But Amos is too tired and sad to eat much.

When bedtime comes, for a long time he can't fall asleep. He lies awake next to Thembi and Pavement, thinking about the full schools that have no room for

him. He feels sadder and sadder.

What if there is no place for me anywhere? he thinks. I will have to stay at home, with the small children and the men who have no jobs. How will I learn anything then?

Two

The next morning, Amos's mother wakes him very early. 'Today, I am not going to work at Mrs Botha's house,' she says. 'I am going to take you to find a school. Dress quickly, Amos.'

They leave Gogo behind to rest her legs, and take the bus to the other side of town.

They try at the first school: 'Sorry, no room here,' they're told.

'Sorry, we are full up,' the second school says.

'Try somewhere else,' advises the third.

It is just like yesterday. We have no luck thinks Amos, holding his suitcase tightly and trying not to cry.

Even his mother is not looking very hopeful any more.

'What are we to do?' his mother later complains to her friend, Mrs Zondi, whose daughter, Promise, is also looking for a school.

'Madiba has said that our children must go to school. But there are not enough schools. So where can we send them?'

'I know a school we can try,' says Mrs Zondi. 'It's that one at the bottom of the valley.'

'I am sure it will be full, like all the others,' Amos's mother sighs.

'No,' says Mrs Zondi. 'This school is empty. It has no pupils in it at all.'

'I know that school!' says an old grandfather, who is standing nearby with his granddaughter.

'It was
closed down
some years
ago, when this
was a Whites Only
neighbourhood, because there
were not enough children here to fill it.'

'There are enough children now!' says Amos's mother. 'Show us where this empty school is. Let's go there.'

They hurry down the steep, hot road together.

Fat Mrs Zondi.

Thin Mrs Gumede.

And the old grandfather in his black suit and hat, with the children skipping behind him.

Other parents see them and want to know where they are going.

'To the school in the valley,' Mrs Zondi shouts back. 'It's standing there empty. Come with us. Bring your children. Come!'

Soon, there is quite a crowd of people

marching
down the
long, steep hill:
mothers, fathers,
children, grandparents.
Even a few dogs.

Some are smartly
dressed. Some are
barefoot. Some have
walking sticks. Some
carry umbrellas for
shade.

Everyone is
talking and
laughing

loudly. They are all excited at the thought that they might have a school for their children at last.

They reach the bottom of the valley. And there is the school, standing all on its own against the hillside. It looks very neglected.

The grass is high around it. Part of the roof has fallen in. There are no doors and no furniture. The windows are full of broken glass.

'Look at this school! It is all broken!' cries one of the mothers, clucking her tongue disappointedly.

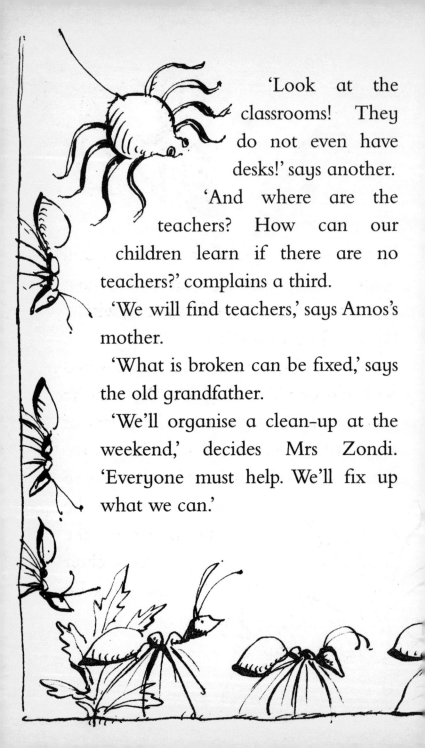

'Look at the classrooms! They do not even have desks!' says another.

'And where are the teachers? How can our children learn if there are no teachers?' complains a third.

'We will find teachers,' says Amos's mother.

'What is broken can be fixed,' says the old grandfather.

'We'll organise a clean-up at the weekend,' decides Mrs Zondi. 'Everyone must help. We'll fix up what we can.'

Amos wanders into one of the empty classrooms. It's very dusty inside. There are weeds growing  up through the floor. There are ants and beetles and spiders everywhere. A broken desk sits on its own in the corner, with a broken chair beside it.

Amos looks at the blackboard, covered with old chalk writing. On the wall he sees the drawings that the last class of children has made. He sees the charts, full of words and pictures. Smiling, he sits down on the broken chair and puts his

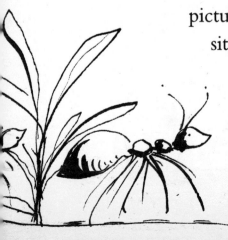

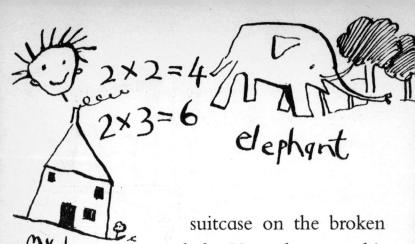

2×2=4
2×3=6

elephant

my house

fish

suitcase on the broken desk. He takes out his pencil and exercise-book and tries to copy the writing on the board.

'I think I would like to be a teacher when I'm big,' he says to

himself. 'Teachers are very clever people. They know a lot of things.'

Three

That weekend, the Gumede family is very busy. They leave home early and walk the long walk down to Amos's school in the valley.

Mrs Gumede carries buckets and wash-rags.

Gogo brings brooms and a dustpan.

Thembi has a mop and scrubbing-brushes.

Amos brings the wheelbarrow and a spade.

Pavement wants to carry something too. So Amos gives him a stick to hold.

They pass some friends, sitting on the pavement, gossiping in the sunshine.

'Where are you going with all those cleaning things?' the friends want to know.

'We're taking them to the school in the valley. We are

going to try
and fix it up
for our children,'
Amos's mother tells
them.

'That will be a lot of work,' the friends say. 'That school is very run-down. We'd better come and help you.'

They get up and follow the Gumedes. Pavement offers them his stick to hold. He is tired of carrying it now.

At the school, they find Mrs Zondi and Promise, Grandfather and Granddaughter, and a few of the other parents. Some have brought planks and a stepladder. They are up on the roof, looking at the damage.

Mrs Zondi, who has a loud voice, is supervising. She makes sure that everyone has a job to do.

Thembi and Gogo pull the weeds out of the classroom floors.

Amos's mother sweeps and washes.

Amos picks up the broken glass and other rubbish from outside and carries it in his wheelbarrow to the rubbish hole that grandfather has dug. Pavement helps him, sitting on the wheelbarrow while Amos pushes.

The wheelbarrow is heavy and the sun is hot, but Amos doesn't mind. He sings a little song to himself. He likes the busy sounds of the cleaning and fixing.

*Bang-bang,
knock-knock,*
go the hammers.
*Swisha-sweep, swisha-
sweep*, go the brooms
and mops.

Iggle-eee, iggle-eee, goes
the squeaky wheel of the
wheelbarrow.

'I know a very good
name for our
school,' says
Mrs Zondi.
'We should call
it "Masakhane",
which means "Let's build
together." ' Amos likes that name a lot.

The clean-up crowd is getting bigger.
More people have come, curious to
know what is happening in the valley.
Some have only come to watch, but Mrs

Zondi's loud voice shouts at them, 'Why are you standing there doing nothing when there's work to be done? Come and help us! If everyone helps, the work will go much quicker.'

A reporter arrives from the newspaper. 'What's going on here?' he wants to know.

'We are trying to fix up this broken school, so that our children will have somewhere to learn,' Mrs Zondi tells him.

'But it's not easy,' sighs Grandfather. 'You see how run-down it is.'

'It needs a lot of repairs. But we have no money to pay for them,' says Amos's mother.

'We have no teachers either,' adds Amos worriedly.

The reporter writes everything down in his notebook. He takes the story in to his newspaper.

'Everyone will read about your problem,' he says. 'Maybe you will be lucky and find people to help you.'

Amos is very impressed. 'A newspaper reporter, that's a clever thing to be,' he says to Pavement. 'I think maybe I would like to do that one day, when I am finished school.'

Four

On Monday, Amos feels very tired from all his hard work on the weekend.

He wants to go on sleeping. But his mother wakes him early. 'Get up, Amos,' she says. 'You must get dressed now. You don't want to be late for your first day of school.'

'But my school isn't ready yet,' says Amos.

'That doesn't matter,' his mother tells him. 'You must still go.'

'We have no teachers. Who will give us our lessons?' Amos wants to know.

'Maybe teachers will come today,' says his mother. 'They will read about Masakhane in the newspaper and they will know they are needed there.'

'Goodbye, Pavement,' Amos says, picking up his suitcase. 'I hope when I come back today I will have something clever to tell you.'

Gogo walks Amos down to his school in the valley. It looks much better than the first time they saw it. The grass is cut. The rubbish is gone.

The classrooms are very clean. There is a new wooden sign outside which says:

MASAKHANE PRIMARY SCHOOL

But the holes in the roof and the broken windows are still there.

The children sit on the floor and wait quietly for their teachers to turn up.

They wait and wait, but no teachers come.

Grandfather tells them stories about the old days. Gogo teaches them a counting song. Amos knows it already.

'Never mind,' says Gogo, when they go home again at lunch-time. 'Maybe tomorrow your teachers will come.'

Amos is too sad to answer her. If I could write, I could write and tell Madiba about our problem, he thinks. Madiba always cares about the troubles of the people. He would help us, I'm sure.

The next day is just like the one before. Amos and the other children wait in the classroom all morning. But no teachers come.

The day after that, it is the same thing. The children are tired of waiting now. They play fighting games and make a lot of noise.

Gogo and the other parents get cross with them. 'We are wasting our time here,' they say to each other. 'No teachers are coming. We might as well take our children home.'

'Wait . . . ' says Amos, looking out of the window. 'Who is this coming?'

The children all run to the doorway to look. Two big black cars are hurrying down the road towards their school. They look very important.

'Maybe these are our teachers at last!' says Amos, hopefully.

'I don't think so,' says Grandfather. 'These are not teachers' cars. Look at the flags. They belong to the government!'

The first car stops by the sign that says MASAKHANE PRIMARY SCHOOL. Men in suits get out. Amos doesn't know them. They open the door of the second car. A man climbs out.

He is tall and thin and a little bit stooped, like a tree that strong winds have blown against.

He is wearing an African shirt of yellow and orange.

His hair is white like Grandfather's.

His face is one that Amos knows well.

He sees the children crowding in the

49

doorway and lifts his hand to them in greeting.

'Madiba!' Gogo cries in amazement. 'That is he, Amos! That is the great Madiba himself!'

The word travels from mouth to mouth, like wind rushing through tree leaves.

'Madiba – it's Madiba – President Nelson Mandela himself is here at our school!'

They all rush outside together.

Mandela walks towards them. He stops in front of Amos, who is in the front. 'I have heard about a school,' he says, 'called Masakhane, which the people are busy fixing up with their own hands. Where the children are so hungry to learn, that they come every day, even though there are no teachers.'

'This is Masakhane, O Madiba,' Amos whispers shyly. 'And we are those children who want to learn.'

Smiling, Madiba nods his head at him. 'Hunger for knowledge is a very good thing,' he says. 'Children who like to

learn will grow up to be wise and clever.'

He looks up at Amos's school. His eyes see everything.

The broken roof.

The missing doors.

The classrooms with nothing inside them.

He sees also the hard work of the people: the cleaned walls, the cut grass, the cleared rubbish.

'People who know how to work hard for what they want deserve support,' he

says. 'It is people like you who will help build our country into a strong country.'

Amos tugs at his sleeve. 'But we have no teachers to teach us, Madiba,' he says. 'Can you help us with that problem?'

'I will speak to the school authorities,' Madiba promises. 'I will tell them to send you teachers, desks, books – everything you need.'

'Will they send them soon?' Amos asks him eagerly.

'You have my word,' Mandela says.

He puts his hand on Amos's head.

His smile feels just like the sun.

Amos looks up into his black eyes.

His face is full of deep lines, like a strong rock that has weathered many harsh storms.

I know now what I want to be when I grow up, thinks Amos. A great leader. A president who is wise and strong and loves his people. Just like Madiba.